MAKOA
AND THE PLACE OF REFUGE

WRITTEN BY
JERRY CUNNYNGHAM

 ISLAND HERITAGE

MAKOA
AND THE PLACE OF REFUGE

Written by Jerry Cunnyngham
Illustrated by Sharon Alshams

Published by
ISLAND HERITAGE
P U B L I S H I N G
A DIVISION OF THE MADDEN CORPORATION
99-880 Iwaena Street
Aiea, Hawaii 96701
(808) 487-7299
E-mail: hawaii4u@pixi.com

ISBN NO. 089610-295-5
First Edition, First Printing – 1997

Jerry Cunnyngham
(1931-1995)

ABOUT THE AUTHOR

Author Jerry Cunnyngham, a teacher from Nevada, fell in love with Hawaii during an extended vacation in Hawaii, and was especially fascinated with the Place of Refuge at Honaunau on the Big Island of Hawaii. This fascination prompted him to write a book concerning this interesting place in Hawaiian history.

The author submitted the story to Island Heritage in June 1994, with a note, "Although the story is fictional, I have spent a great deal of time in order to make the background authentic." The fictional story, set in old Hawaii, is about a boy approaching manhood who breaks a kapu (taboo) by entering the burial place of a king.

Forced to flee to the Place of Refuge at Honaunau, the young man experiences a number of adventures, from warriors who pursue him to wild boars and sharks ... and a lovely young lady who helps him when he is injured.

Our editors and reviewers fell in love with Makoa and the Place of Refuge. Following our annual manuscript review, we notified the author that we wanted to publish Makoa. Unfortunately, Jerry Cunnyngham had died the previous month. His widow, Geneie, worked with us to bring his dream to reality...

As a tribute to the author, it is with great pleasure that Island Heritage Publishing presents Makoa and the Place of Refuge as the first book in a series, Adventures in Hawaii, for middle school readers. We hope, with the publication of this book, that young people of today will cherish the rich cultural history Hawaii has to offer . . . and appreciate the courage and dynamics of the Hawaiians of yesteryear.

— Island Heritage Publishing

ACKNOWLEDGMENTS

My heartfelt thanks to the people who advised me on this book.

Special thanks to Yoshi and Artyce Terada for the use of their library on Hawaiiana.

Mahalo nui loa to the haunting mystique surrounding the Pu'uhonua o Honaunau (Place of Refuge at Honaunau) which prompted me to write this book.

— J.C.

AUTHOR'S NOTE

The ancient people of Hawai'i were governed by a system of rigid laws or bans called kapus. These kapus were easy to break and the penalty was often death. To counteract such harshness, the priests instituted places of refuge where a kapu breaker could find sanctuary. These safe houses were set up at various places throughout the islands. Although this story is fictional, it portrays what could have happened had someone broken a big kapu...someone like Makoa, a boy fast approaching manhood.

CONTENTS

Illustrations:
Page 5, 18, 36, 50, 66, 75, 85, and 89.

Dedicated to all those
who seek a Place of Refuge

BROKEN KAPU

Makoa lived in Hawai'i long before the explorers, missionaries and tourists intruded on his island home. Makoa was born near the village of Pumaluu on the windward side of Hawai'i, the largest island in the Hawaiian chain. Many years later, the same big island would give birth to Kamehameha, the greatest warrior king in Hawaiian history.

Like all the other young people on the oscillate, Makoa was brought up to respect the ancient ways of his Polynesian ancestors—men and women who sailed to Hawaii in huge double-hulled sailing canoes from other Pacific islands. He was taught to obey all of the island's kapus which were strict bans or no-no's regulating social

1

and religious behavior. Since death was the price for breaking most kapus, the village kahuna (priest) would from time to time teach the young people about what was forbidden...kapu.

During one such time, on a sparkling afternoon, Makoa, along with a dozen other young people, sat cross-legged in a small coconut palm grove just outside their village. The boys wore malos, loincloths of printed kapa cloth. The girls were clad in short, brightly colored skirts. Flower leis of all the rainbow colors adorned their graceful, bronze-colored necks.

All eyes were on the kahuna as he spoke.

"It is kapu to enter the burial place of a king...obey or die! It is kapu to touch or remove any objects from a royal burial place...obey or die!"

"It is kapu to touch or remove any stones from a heiau (temple)...obey or die!"

"It is kapu to carry bananas aboard a boat..obey or die!"

"It is kapu for a female to eat bananas...obey or die!"

"It is kapu..."

As the old priest chanted a seemingly endless litany of kapus, Makoa's eyes momentarily scanned the tops of the heavily laden palm trees. It seemed to Makoa that there were more kapus than the coconuts clustered above them.

2

Listening to rules forbidding this and forbidding that was hard to take on such a beautiful rainbow day. But out of respect for the old kahuna, Makoa at least feigned attention. His eyes were fixed on the priest but his mind was fishing, swimming, surfing and playing a warrior version of the hunter and hunted game with his best friend, Kakani.

Out of the corner of his eye, he sneaked a glance at his friend. Kakani seemed absorbed in the kahuna's words. But Makoa knew better. Kakani's mind, like his own, was also at play.

Finally, the old kahuna grew winded and dismissed everyone.

"At last," Makoa said to Kakani, "I thought the kahuna would not stop talking until the sun dipped into the sea."

"Ahh, but the sun is still hanging in the sky," Kakani said, "...Time enough to play at least one good game of hunter and hunted, eh, my friend?"

After a quick glance at the sky, Makoa nodded. "Yes, plenty of time for one game."

"I believe it is your turn to be hunted," Kakani said.

"Then start counting...and good luck to you in finding me, but better luck to me in hiding."

So saying, Makoa laughed—then ran off to hide. Kakani usually found Makoa, but only after a long intensive search. This time Makoa did not want to be found at all. He wanted Kakani to give up. Instead of heading toward the forest west of the village, as he always did, he ran toward the cliff overlooking the ocean.

Kakani counted by beating on a hollow log drum. As Makoa ran along the cliff side, he heard the drum beat—Slow counts at first, just as it should be; but toward the end of the count, the beats were much faster. Even though his friend was cheating, Makoa smiled, for he had done the same thing himself.

When the drum quit beating, Makoa stopped running. He looked all around for a place to hide but there was not one good place in sight. Just as he started to turn away from the cliff, he spied a tangle of rope-like vines hanging over the edge of the cliff. When he peeked over the edge, he saw that the vines trailed all the way down to a rocky beach. With the prospect of a good hiding place, Makoa grabbed hold of the vines and lowered himself down the steep sides of the cliff. Half-way down, he spotted the mouth of a cave almost hidden behind the vines.

"This cave will make a good hiding place," Makoa thought.

But as soon as he entered the cave, he knew he was in a forbidden place...a place of kapu. It was obviously a burial place of a very important person. A skeleton wrapped in kapa cloth lay on

4

a wooden platform. The exposed skull bore a yellow feathered helmet.

The body was surrounded by treasures of all kinds. There were finely carved bowls and jars made of monkey pod wood; small god images of koa wood; and leis made of shells, feathers and seeds. Capes fashioned from the beautiful feathers of the mamo and 'i'iwi birds lined the walls of the cave. There were so many of the precious capes that Makoa suspected he was in the burial place of a king. His suspicion was soon confirmed when he spied two crossed kapu sticks, the symbol of royalty, leaning against the north wall of the cave.

And then Makoa's eyes fell on the war clubs of the dead king. They rested in a bamboo rack beside the burial platform. There were a dozen clubs, but one stood out above all the rest. It was made of dark shiny wood with beautifully carved god figures on the handle. The head was ball shaped and studded with shark's teeth.

Makoa's heart pounded like the surf as he studied the club. He had never seen or even heard of such a club as this one.

"I have already broken a sacred kapu by entering the cave," he reasoned. "Surely I can do no more harm by just touching the club."

So Makoa gingerly pressed his finger tips against the carved handle. A chill of excitement ran up his spine. But he was not satisfied with merely touching the war club. He removed it from the rack and held it in his hand. Power seemed to serge through his body. He felt like a king. Then he lifted the war club and swung it high above his head. He was a king. He was a king in combat. He was a king defending his island empire. He was a king conquering other islands.

Makoa was so carried away by his imagination that he yelled out several ear splitting war cries. Moments later, Kakani entered the cave. When he saw Makoa with the war club in his hand, he shouted, "Makoa, what are you doing? Have you lost your mind?"

Makoa said nothing. He was too stunned to speak.

Kakani looked all around the cave. "Makoa, you have broken a very great kapu. This is the place of a king. His spirit will be angry with you. Put that war club back where it belongs and leave right now, wikiwiki (hurry)."

"But it is such a wonderful club," Makoa protested, "And there are so many of them here. Surely his spirit will not miss one small war club."

"You know better than that, Makoa. Everything in this cave belongs to his spirit. The club is a part of that spirit."

Makoa stroked the club tenderly and said, "I cannot part with it, Kakani. I have never owned such a treasure as this before."

Kakani frowned. "And you do not own this treasure now, either. It belongs to his spirit...put it back!"

"But I have already broken a kapu by entering the cave and touching the club. And you too, Kakani, have also broken a kapu."

Kakani stared at the wrapped skeleton. "I know I have broken a kapu, but his spirit will understand that my heart did not mean to do such a thing. And his spirit will also understand if you place the war club back where it belongs and leave."

Makoa knew in his heart that Kakani spoke the truth. But the war club in his hand made him feel like a king. He had never felt that way before.

"I cannot put the club back, Kakani. I must keep it."

Kakani shook his head sadly. "Then I will have no part of what you do. I will not tell on you because you are my friend, but I will no longer share time with you." Then Kakani left the cave. Makoa stared after his friend. He understood how Kakani felt, but he didn't think his friend understood about the war club. Makoa rubbed his hand on the club and after awhile the cave grew dark. Suddenly a cold wind came rushing off the ocean causing the wooden bowls and jars to whistle. Makoa was frightened. He tucked the war club in the waistband of his black and brown malo, then climbed the cliff and ran home.

▼△▽△▼△▽△▼△▽△▼△▽△▼△

RUN
FOR THE
PLACE OF
REFUGE

▼△▽△▼△▽△▼△▽△▼△▽△▼△

When Makoa reached home, he wrapped the war club in kapa cloth, then hid it in the canoe shed next to the house. He did not tell his parents what he had done. That night a strong wind came whistling from the windward side of the island. Makoa's house rattled like dry seeds in a gourd. The roof fluttered like a giant bird ready to take flight.

Makoa and his parents were filled with fear. While his mother and father desperately prayed before their crude, wooden house god, Makoa sneaked off to the canoe shed. Before the king's war club he fell on his knees and shouted above the wind, "Please spare my family, O Great King! I swear on the spirits of my ancestors to return your club as soon as the sun shows itself!"

But the following morning the weather was so rough Makoa could not leave the house. Fierce winds continued to strike Makoa's village, this time accompanied by a pelting rain. And to add to the misery, wild boars from the hills came down to the village killing pigs, dogs and chickens. Some of them even chased children about. Early in the evening the wind died down only to be followed by frightful earth tremors.

Makoa was convinced that Pele, goddess of fire and volcanoes, was punishing the village because he had broken a great kapu. As if to confirm that belief, a nearby volcano erupted shortly before midnight, spilling crimson lava down its sides.

After many hours in prayer, the village kahuna blew three long mournful blasts on his conch shell. This was a signal for all the people to gather in the Temple Compound, now lit with a ring of torches. In a very short time the place was filled with a crowd of screaming, frightened men, women and children. Two dozen warriors in full battle dress quieted the people so the old priest could be heard.

Lifting his arms towards the volcano, the kahuna prayed in a trembling, yet loud voice.

"O Great Pele, goddess of fire and volcanoes, what have we done to displease you?"

So saying, the kahuna listened for an answer. Everyone waited nervously, their eyes darting back and forth from the kahuna to the belching volcano. After a long wait, a great rush of wind passed over the kahuna causing his brown face to turn white as coconut meat.

"Auweee!!!" he shouted. "One of us has broken a great kapu! The goddess Pele is very angry!"

The villagers looked at one another anxiously, wondering who it was that had broken the great kapu. Kakani stared at Makoa but he did not give his friend away. Makoa was ashamed of himself. The whole village was paying for his sin. He wanted very much to confess and spare his village from Pele's wrath. But he could not talk...fear had paralyzed his tongue.

Then all of a sudden the villagers all pointed to the volcano and screamed. A river of blood red lava was flowing straight toward their village. Makoa could stand his fear no longer. He ran to the canoe shed and seized the war club. Then he raced back to the meeting place and laid it at the feet of the kahuna.

"I am the one who broke the great kapu. I took this war club from a king's burial place," he pointed toward the sea, "a cave on the side of a cliff."

The crowd was stunned, Makoa's family

shamed, and the kahuna horrified.

"You must return the war club immediately!" the priest shouted.

With a quick nod, Makoa picked up the club and dashed toward the cliffs. But just as he cleared his village, the lava flow suddenly turned away from it. When Makoa reached the cliff, his heart jumped in his throat. The lava had spilled over the edge of the cliff and sealed the cave entrance.

With a heavy heart Makoa trudged back to the temple compound. When he told the kahuna what had happened, the priest became very angry and yelled at him.

"You have done a terrible thing to the king's spirit! You have done a terrible thing to your village! You have done a terrible thing to yourself! Go home! Tomorrow I will decide your fate!"

As Makoa left the temple grounds, the people all turned their backs on him as if he himself was kapu. Only Makoa's parents and Kakani dared to look upon him. Kakani had told Makoa that he would not share time with him, but when he saw his friend in such terrible trouble he could not bring himself to abandon him. Just after midnight Kakani secretly visited Makoa.

"The penalty for breaking such a kapu, as you have broken," Kakani said, "is death."

"Yes, I know that," Makoa answered.

"The kahuna will order the Temple guards to bind your hands and feet."

"Yes, I know that."

"Then he will lay your head upon a flat rock."

"Yes, yes, I know that."

"And then," Kakani continued, "he will beat out your brains with a very big club."

Makoa nodded, "I know, I know."

"A club five times bigger than the one you stole from the dead king's burial place."

"You need not remind me of that, my friend," Makoa said in exasperation. "It was only three months ago that we watched the kahuna club poor Keino to death in front of the temple steps...remember?"

Kakani nodded. "Yes—and his kapu was not half as bad as the one you just broke."

"Thanks for reminding me, Kakani."

"I am only trying to point out that you have but one chance to live."

"I know that, too," Makoa snapped. "I must get myself to a place of refuge."

"The closest one is but a half day's journey from here," said Kakani.

"I know," Makoa said, "but my kapu is so great that I must seek the highest ranking of the sanctuaries. And that is the Sacred Place of Refuge at Honaunau."

"But that is on the other side of the island. It is a far and difficult journey."

"I am aware of that, Kakani, but my mind is fixed."

"What do you really know of this refuge, anyway?" Kakani asked.

"The kahuna has talked enough about this place. And, unlike you, I paid attention to those talks."

The words of the old priest suddenly flashed in his mind and he recited them to Kakani.

'Pu'uhonua O Honaunau is a sacred place, a gift from the gods to the common people. Those who break a kapu flee there to escape punishment. The Pu'uhonua sits on a small arm of land sticking out into the sea. A large wooden temple, a few houses for the priest and several small huts are the only buildings there. The sacred place is located on the Kona Coast, the leeward side of the island. A 12-foot high rock wall protects the city's landward side. The seaward side is left open. Once inside the wall, a law breaker is safe and protected by the sacred temple. Not even a king can enter it to punish anyone.'

"You repeated his words well, Makoa. And since the kahuna did not put you in a bamboo cage until your execution, then he has given you a chance to run for a place of refuge. But when the sun peeks over the water, the kahuna's warriors will come for you. And when they find that you have fled, then they will pursue you with blood in their eyes and spears in their hands...so you must get yourself a head start on them now—wikiwiki!"

"You are right, Kakani. Wait for me at the potato patch while I say goodbye to my parents."

All this time Makoa's mother and father had been listening to the boys near an open window. By the time Makoa entered the house his mother had already prepared food for this journey—dried fish, sweet potatoes, sugar cane to chew and a green coconut for drinking. It was all wrapped and tied in banana leaves and fitted with a shoulder sling. Tears rolled down her cheeks as she gave the parcel to Makoa. "My heart will be heavy until you are safe."

His father said, "I am going with you, my son."

"No, Father, please, you must stay and take care of Mama. Besides, I need you to sit at a window with a coconut lamp so the warriors will see that you are still here and so I must be, too."

Reluctantly, Makoa's father agreed to stay and let his son go off by himself.

"Aloha," his parents cried as they hugged him. "May the gods protect you."

"Aloha," Makoa said, then slipped quietly out the back door.

When Makoa reached the sweet potato patch west of the village, Kakani said to him, "Wikiwiki, Makoa! The night is more than half gone. You must be on your way!"

"I am ready," Makoa replied, tapping the food package and the war club.

"Dare you take the kapu war club with you?" asked Kakani.

"Yes, I must show it to the great kahuna at the Place of Refuge. Only then will he truly know what I have done."

"Very well, my friend. Now go—and go quickly!"

"But first tell me, what is the shortest, easiest, most obvious route to the Pu'uhonua O Honaunau?"

Kakani was surprised at such a foolish question.

"Why everyone knows that. The shortest, easiest, most obvious way is to skirt south of the two volcanoes, Mauna Loa and her little sister, Kilauea, as you head west to the Kona coast."

"That is correct. Now listen to me very carefully. I am going to Honaunau...to the Place of Refuge. My route is south of Mauna Loa and Kilauea. If the kahuna asks you, tell him what I just said...then you will not be lying."

Kakani smiled. "Now I understand."

As they grasped each other's forearms Kakani said, "And now my friend, the great hide

and seek begins, eh? May the gods go with you."

"Mahalo (thanks), Kakani. Mahalo for being my friend. And now, watch me as I leave."

Makoa headed south, but stopped when he was still within speaking distance. Because of the fiery glow from the volcano, which lit up the entire sky, Kakani could still see his friend. Makoa called back to Kakani, "Tell the kahuna what you just saw me do! Now turn your back on me and leave. Aloha!"

Kakani did as Makoa said. Although he was sad to see him go, Kakani smiled, for he knew what his friend had in mind.

Makoa waited until Kakani was out of sight, then reversed his route and headed north. He would skirt the two volcanoes alright, but from the north—the longest, hardest and least obvious route to the Place of Refuge at Honaunau Bay.

'AKOLU
(THREE)

FALSE TRAIL

Without pausing to rest or eat, Makoa hurried northward. He wanted to cover as much ground as possible before the sun showed itself. When that happened, the temple warriors would be on his trail like a hunter after a wild pig. For awhile, he thought, his false maneuver might fool them, but eventually he knew they would get wise to his trick and then backtrack after him. By that time though, he would have gained precious time and distance...or so he hoped. Time and distance, time and distance—the words gnawed at his brain. Just before the sun was ready to rise, Makoa grew lung tired and leg weary. He finally paused to rest against a candle nut tree. "I will close my eyes for just a little while," he promised himself.

When the sun peeked over the ocean rim at Makoa's village, the kahuna sent warriors to Makoa's house. Not finding him there, they searched the village. When they couldn't find him anywhere, they reported back to the kahuna. The old priest threw back his cape, rubbed his chin thoughtfully, then said, "Find his friend Kakani. I am sure he can tell us where Makoa has gone."

Moments later a nervous Kakani, flanked on both sides by a spear carrying warrior, was escorted up the temple steps to face the kahuna.

"Tell me, Kakani, do you know the penalty for lying to your priest?"

Kakani shook his head up and down vigorously. "Yes, kahuna, I know the penalty."

"That is good because I am going to ask you some questions and I want you to tell me the truth. Look into my eyes when you answer me."

"Yes, kahuna."

"Did your friend Makoa tell you where he was going?"

"Yes, kahuna."

"Where is that?"

"He said he was going to Honaunau...to the Place of Refuge." Kakani pointed westward.

The priest looked deeply into the boy's eyes.

"Good. Now, did he tell you which way he was going?"

"Yes, kahuna."

"Which way was that?"

"He said his route would be south of Mauna Loa and Kilauea."

Again the priest searched Kakani's eyes and was satisfied. "Good. Now, did you actually see your friend leave for the Place of Refuge?"

"Yes, kahuna."

"Which way did he go?"

"I saw him head south."

"With your very own eyes?" the kahuna asked as he stared deeply into Kakani's eyes.

"With my very own eyes," Kakani answered truthfully.

Flashing a wide smile, the kahuna patted Kakani on the shoulders. "I know you have spoken the truth. You may go home, Kakani."

After dismissing the boy, the kahuna ordered six warriors to give chase to Makoa, charging them to "Bring him back alive if you can. If not, then kill him where he stands!"

As the warriors raced away, heading south, the priest sighed heavily. Part of him, the fatherly part, wanted Makoa to reach the Place of Refuge and find forgiveness. The other part of him, the kahuna part, wanted justice done. Makoa had broken a kapu and it was a kahuna's duty to see that the boy was punished for it. The kahuna had not made the law; that was done for him hundreds of years ago. His responsibility was to see that the kapus were enforced whether he thought them just or not. When the warriors were out of sight, the kahuna went into the temple and prayed.

With sweat pouring down his face, Makoa woke with a start. When he saw the sun, hours old already, he jumped to his feet, angry with himself.

"What a fool I am to have fallen asleep like that. Whatever advantage I had with my trick maneuver is lost now."

Shaking his head in disgust, he ran northward, mumbling to himself.

By the time the sun was directly overhead Makoa had moved from a lush, tropical area into a barren, lava bed region. Here he stopped to refresh himself in a small lava cave. While he lunched on dried fish and coconut milk, his pursuers were at that very moment backtracking after him. They were both angry and ashamed at being tricked by a boy not yet old enough o be a warrior.

Makoa did not linger after his meager meal. He was up running and thinking of ways to slow down his pursuers. He realized that as a boy he could not match the warriors' strength and endurance. He had to rely on his wits.

As he ran over the lava beds, he chewed on a stub piece of sugar cane and centered his thoughts on a certain trick he had played on Kakani while playing the hunter and hunted game. After clearing the lava beds, Makoa entered a stretch of small ground ferns and bushes. Here he stopped to put his plan into action.

First he walked westward, careful not to leave any tell tale tracks. Occasionally he would snap a twig on a bush and allow a fern stem to be bent. His idea was to make his trail traceable, but only to trained eyes...like those of his pursuers. After traveling this way for a quarter of a mile, he made a wide arc to the north, making sure he left no signs whatsoever. Then he backtracked to the original spot where he had marked the trail. At this point, he turned and walked northward for a quarter of a mile making sure that any untrained eye could follow the trail. He threw down pieces of chewed sugar cane and dried fish. He dripped coconut milk onto the fern leaves. He snapped branches on the bushes and trampled ferns so it appeared as if a dozen warriors had rushed that way.

Satisfied that the trail northward was so obviously marked that a blind person could follow it, Makoa made a wide arc. Again he was careful not to leave any signs. He then back-tracked to the original spot where he had marked the two trails.

After a short prayer he headed south, back to the lava beds. Here he turned west and followed alongside the faintly marked trail while staying track proof on the bare, hard lava beds.

If his plan worked, Makoa thought, the war-riors would be confused by the two dead end trails; and that confusion would give him some time. If the plan failed, however, then he would have wasted precious time and his pursuers would profit from his dumb mistake.

It was late afternoon and Makoa was still moving on lava beds when he came upon a clus-ter of 'ohelo berries, the bright red berries sacred to Pele. Growing out of lava cracks, they appeared as an offering from the goddess. In more than one of his talks, the kahuna had said the 'ohelo berries could be eaten, but only after a gift of the berries was first offered to Pele.

Makoa knelt alongside the berries and counted as he picked them. He used his loin cloth to collect the fruit. Makoa figured half the berries would be an appropriate gift to Pele but threw in several more just to be on the safe side. Using small flat lava rocks, he fashioned a small shrine for the goddess. He placed her share of berries in a neat pile on a miniature altar. Then lifting his arms, he prayed out loud, "Mahalo, Pele-honua-mea (Pele of the sacred earth), mahalo for the berries. And please help me to reach the Sacred Place of Refuge."

Makoa then wolfed down his berries and continued on his way, smacking his red stained lips. An hour before sundown he left the lava beds and turned north. A short run brought him to a narrow valley forested by giant tree ferns. He entered the forest, then headed westward. Although the sun had not yet kissed the sea, it was already dark and gloomy inside the forest.

Makoa had intended on running and walking far into the night, but his lungs and legs could carry him no longer. Too tired to eat or drink, he crawled beneath some large fern fronds. Then, placing the club and food near his side, he rolled onto his stomach. Completely exhausted, he fell asleep as soon as his head hit the soft, fern matted ground.

'AHA
(FOUR)

▽△▽△▽△▽△▽△▽△▽△▽

LITTLE
PARADISE

▽△▽△▽△▽△▽△▽△▽△▽

Before the sun had set, the six pursuing warriors had reached the starting point of Makoa's two dead end trails. Mookini, the best spearsman on the island and self appointed leader of the pursuers, toyed with his shark tooth necklace as he considered the two trails. Well over six feet tall, he was an impressive figure of a man. His tattooed face wore a perpetual scowl; similar to the ones found on the fierce god images that surrounded Sacred Temples. Although he was obviously a man to be feared, he respected courage and intelligence in others...even his enemies.

"This Makoa is indeed a wise one for his young years," Mookini said to his warriors. "He fooled us when he pretended to go south of the two volcanoes. Now he is trying to fool us again with this false trail that leads to the west. It is a trail made by a boy wise enough to conceal his tracks, yet inexperienced enough to leave signs. All believable and logical."

Mookini pointed to the other trail. "But see how he has made the trail northward such an easy path to follow. Pieces of fish and sugar cane litter the trail."

"Yes," the shortest warrior responded, "and he has dripped coconut milk on both sides of the trail to make it easier to follow."

"And see how he has clumsily trampled the ferns and bent the twigs on bushes," another warrior added.

"A blind man could follow this trail," someone mumbled.

"The boy we track is much too wise to make such a childishly marked trail...not without a devious reason in mind," Mookini said. "Makoa would have us believe that he went westward. Ha! It is obvious that he took this trickster-marked trail northward thinking we would not believe him to be so foolish. But in trying to trick us, he has out tricked himself. We will go north-ward also."

"Let us go after him now!" they all shouted.

Mookini pointed his spear to the sky. "No, the sun is bidding us farewell. We will rest here and start fresh when it bids us good morning."

At first Makoa thought it was sunlight streaking through the fern fronds, but no, it was moonlight...pale white slivers of moonlight. Was it this light, he thought, that had awakened him from a deep sleep? While he wondered over this, a mournful cry raised the hairs on his arms and legs. At first he thought it might be the wind whistling through the fern fronds. But the air was still as rocks. While he puzzled over the mysterious sound, it came again, this time louder and closer...so close he could swear it was right next to his side. As he bent his head and strained to listen, a third cry pierced the night air. There was no doubt about it. The mystery sound—a mournful, moaning cry—was coming from a spot right next to him. For protection, he reached out for the wrapped war club. As soon as he removed the kapa covering, a much louder wailing cry assailed his ears.

"The war club," Makoa gasped. "It is the war club that is crying to me!"

Makoa got on his knees and promised the dead king's spirit he would turn the club over to the great kahuna as soon as he reached the place of refuge. But no amount of promises would silence the club's cries.

Makoa tried burying the club under a pile of dead fronds, but it did little good. Finally, when he could stand the club's wailing no longer, he used the kapu club to dig a deep hole. Then he buried it beneath a foot of red dirt.

As he lay down, thoroughly exhausted, he listened. Not nearly as loud, Makoa thought, but he could still hear the club crying to him. In desperation, he collected a fistful of pulu, the soft, silky fibers that cover the fronds of young tree ferns. He wadded the pulu into two small balls, then stuffed one in each ear.

The talking war club's voice was muffled enough for Makoa to sleep but it wasn't a sound, restful sleep. All night long he tossed and turned. When the first ray of sunshine beamed on his camp, he dug up the war club and was more than eager to be on his way.

He continued westward, staying in the narrow forest valley of tree ferns. As he walked, he breakfasted on cold fish and drank the last of the green coconut. Along the way he found several kinds of fruits and berries which greatly relieved the monotony of the dried fish.

The further west he travelled, the more dense was the forest of tree ferns, so much so that he moved under a thick canopy of foliage. Stingy rays of sunlight stabbed at the valley floor, guiding his way like kukui torches. When the sunbeams were straight up and down, he stopped to lunch on dried fish and berries. In a brief moment he was up and running, anxious to put as much time and distance between his pursuers and himself. Time and distance, time and distance...

Had he known how strongly his pursuers had fallen for his false trail trick, Makoa would have breathed easier. The warriors had followed the northern trail five miles past the point Makoa had quit marking it. They were convinced that they would eventually pick it up again and that this dry trail was just one more of the boy's wily tricks. It was only after reaching a tiny village of banana eaters that they realized Makoa had duped them again. The villagers all swore they had not seen a boy of Makoa's description pass their way.

Confused, angry and determined, the warriors, led by a snarling Mookini, backtracked to pick up Makoa's trail...the true one.

Toward late afternoon, while running through a particularly dense part of the forest, Makoa heard noises. When he stopped to listen more intently, he heard soft gurgling sounds like those made by a baby. He followed the sounds until they brought him to a small clearing. Makoa's tense face softened immediately when he saw a baby waterfall, scarcely taller than himself, cascading gently over a wall of basalt rocks. The silver ribbon of water, catching a sun leak in the forest roof, fed a darkened pool that mirrored the green ferns and red ferns surrounding it.

The miniature waterfall brought to Makoa's mind stories of the menehune, a legendary race of small people. According to what he had been told, they were great builders of canoes, fish ponds, and temples, to name but a few. Looking all around the clearing, Makoa thought, "Surely this would be a place the little people would love to live. It is a little paradise and that is what I will call it...Little Paradise."

Thirsty after a long day of walking and running, Makoa laid down his war club and food package. Then he knelt beside the pool and drank deeply of the cool, dark water. While drinking, he noticed the presence of crayfish on the pool's sandy bottom. Using two fingers as tongs, he extricated a half dozen of the fattest ones. Then after pinching off their tails and removing the crusts, he ate them raw. The sweet, tender meat was a much welcomed and needed treat.

Satisfied, Makoa sat propped against a tree trunk near the pool. For a long time he allowed himself to be swallowed up by the beauty of the place. Everything about Little Paradise enchanted him—the sights, the sounds, the smell...then all of a sudden Makoa's nose twitched. Up until this time, Little Paradise had made his head reel with the sweet, intoxicating aroma of flowers numbering like the stars. But now a different smell attacked his nostrils...wild, thick, sinking and strong enough to overpower the sweet smelling flowers of Little Paradise.

Makoa did not have to hear or see the cause of it.

"Pua'a!" he said aloud, "and a wild one!"

▽△▽△▽△▽△▽△▽△▽△

BATTLE WITH A WILD PIG

▽△▽△▽△▽△▽△▽△▽△

The words had scarcely left his lips when a short series of deep guttural snorts and grunts confirmed his identification. Before Makoa could get to his feet, a wild bristling boar rushed from out of the underbrush and into the clearing. Just short of a spear's length of Makoa, he came to a sudden stop.

Slowly and very carefully, Makoa rose to his feet. All the while the grayish-black boar kept his close-set beady eyes fixed on him. Makoa stood, frozen for the moment. The war club was lying on the ground but too far away to be of help.

As Makoa's mind tried to figure a way out, the boar grew impatient. His bushy eyebrows began twitching and his lower jaw, armed with two powerful tusks, started slobbering. All the signs pointed to an attack, Makoa thought. Imminent danger spurred Makoa's wily brain into action. The pool, he reasoned, would give him some time. He would jump in the water as soon as the boar attacked, then try to get hold of the war club.

As he planned his course of action, the boar shook his broad head from side to side, raising a cloud of flies and gnats that lived off his crusty hide. And then all of a sudden, with eyes shining like black pearls, the boar charged.

It only took Makoa four bats of any eye to reach the pool. He jumped in as far as he could go. The pool was only knee deep, but deep enough, Makoa hoped, to slow the boar and give him a chance to get the war club. The force of the jump drove Makoa calf deep into the pool's sandy bottom. Panic stricken, he yelled as he wiggled himself free then waded toward the far end of the pool where the club lay. Makoa had no sooner freed himself when the huge boar belly-flopped onto the water causing a minor tidal wave. Makoa slipped as he reached shore and was on his hands and knees when the boar caught up with him. Using his left tusk as a dagger, the boar made a quick upward thrust into the back of Makoa's upper left arm.

"Auweee!" Makoa yelled. Then pain and

fear made him jump from the pool. His first inclination was to run but when he saw the boar slipping, unable to pull himself from the pool, he changed his mind. Instead of running Makoa grabbed the war club and whacked the boar on his leathery snout. The wild pig squealed as blood spurted out onto Makoa's loincloth. The boy whacked him once more, this time on the top of his thick, broad head. The boar squealed again, but much louder. Afraid that pain and fear would do the same for the boar as it had for him, Makoa ran to the waterfall and climbed to the top of the rock wall.

Once on top he tore a strip from his loin-cloth and bound his wound. Then he squatted down with the club in his hand to wait for the boar. He did not have long to wait. With a great deal of grunting and snorting, the big boar heaved himself from the pool. At that moment, Makoa promised himself he would never eat pig again.

Standing with his feet wide apart, the soak-ing-wet boar shot his head from side to side. Despite his position on top of the wall, Makoa was showered by the downpour. Then, with mincing steps, the hunter paced back and forth in front of the wall. His beady eyes were fixed on the hunted. His eyes were no longer shining like black pearls but burning like hot coals.

With the boar's head tilted up at him, Makoa was able to get a good long look at the boar's dagger tusks. The sight made him tremble. Makoa's father had once told him that animals could smell fear on humans. Makoa was certain the boar could smell his fear and was enjoying it.

After teasing Makoa for a long time, the boar suddenly stood up on his hind legs and leaned against the rock wall. His front hooves reached the top of the wall as did most of his head. Excited at being so close to his quarry, the boar grunted and snorted so much his jowls quivered like freshly made poi.

Again, fear gave Makoa courage. With both hands on the club, he gave the boar two quick whacks right between the eyes. With a chorus of grunts, snorts and squeals, he staggered from Little Paradise with not so much as a backward glance.

When Makoa was convinced that the boar had gone for good, he climbed down from the rock wall. Right away he fell to his knees and lifted the war club toward the sky, "Mahalo, spirit of the dead king," he cried, "Mahalo for allowing me to use your club against the boar."

After praying, he felt dizzy but would not rest until he had cleaned the war club. He used sand from the bottom of the pool to scrub the weapon until it glistened. Then he bathed his wound and re-bandaged it. Still feeling faint, he drank deeply from the pool and then fell asleep with the war club clutched tightly in his fist.

While Makoa had been fighting the boar, his pursuers had picked up his trail. When they tried to enter the same forest Makoa had entered the previous evening, they were intercepted by a band of Pig-Eater warriors. Mookini and his men were then escorted north to the Pig-Eater's village. In front of the local temple they were presented first to the chief and then the kahuna.

"Why are you trespassing on our territory armed with war clubs and spears?" the chief demanded.

Mookini spoke for the pursuers, "Forgive our intrusion on your land, O Mighty Chief of the Pig Eaters. Our war clubs and spears are not meant for your people but one of our own...a boy called Makoa. He has broken a very great kapu and is at this very moment on his way to the Pu'uhonua O Honaunau. We are trying to stop him so we can bring him to justice."

The chief discussed Mookini's words with his kahuna. After a short time, the kahuna asked Mookini, "What kapu did this Makoa break?"

"He stole a war club from a king's burial place," Mookini replied.

Shocked, the chief and the kahuna both

sucked air at the same time.

"You are truly on a sacred mission," the kahuna said gravely.

"And we will help you with both food and trackers," the chief added. "Mahalo," Mookini said, bowing his head to each man, "Mahalo."

As Mookini turned to go, the kahuna said, "But we cannot help you until we have celebrated the feast day of our village god. The celebration begins this very evening and will not end until tomorrow evening. Of course you will be our guests and help us honor our god."

Mookini and his men were disappointed. If they accepted this invitation they would lose a day and a night chasing Makoa. On the other hand, if they refused the kahuna's invitation they might end up as offerings to the Pig Eater's god.

Sick at heart, but smiling, Mookini bowed to the kahuna. "We look forward to honoring your god."

'AONO
(SIX)

MAKAOLA

For the first few hours, Makoa slept the sleep of a warrior after a fierce battle, but then in the middle of the night he grew restless. When he stirred himself awake, he discovered that he was burning up with a fever. His whole body was hot even though the night air in Little Paradise was cool and refreshing. His arm throbbed with pain. When he felt it, it seemed hotter than the rest of his body. Painful as it was to move, he managed to drag his body to the pool's edge and drink from it. The cool water felt so good he dunked his fevered head beneath it several times before pulling away. Refreshed for the moment, he fell asleep—but it was a restless, tortured sleep full of weird, meaningless dreams.

Makoa thought he was still dreaming when he awoke to see a girl standing in the clearing. She wore a short, flowered skirt and a bright red cape. Her slender golden-brown body was enveloped in a single sun ray that beamed down through the overhanging ferns.

Makoa raised on his elbows and strained his eyes to look at her. She was the most beautiful girl he had ever seen. Long black hair, shiny with coconut oil, cascaded around her shoulders. And above her right ear she had fixed a fiery red flower.

Surely this must be Pele herself, thought Makoa. She is young but Pele can take the form of any female she chooses—a young maiden, or an old woman, Makoa reasoned.

When the girl saw Makoa's bandaged arm, she hurried to his side and knelt down.

"Are you Pele?" Makoa asked in a quivering voice.

The girl laughed as she fussed with the bandage knot. "No, I am not Pele. Why should you ask that?"

"Because you are beautiful like a goddess, and that red cape you are wearing is the color of bleeding lava...Pele's color."

"I am sorry to disappoint you," she smiled. "But I am neither Pele nor any other goddess. My name is Makaola. It means happy in the language of my ancestors. They come from the fifteen stars in the ocean (Cook Islands)."

She smiled again. "I am but a mere mortal from the Village of the Pig Eaters...just north of here."

"A pig is the cause of my injury," Makoa said, "I only wish your people could have eaten him before I reached this place." He laughed, but it sounded more like a moan.

Makaola looked all around the clearing. "And where is this pig now?"

Makoa puffed out his chest. "I beat him away with this..."

All of a sudden he realized his mistake and tried to cover the war club.

"Oh, I already know about the kapu club...and you too, Makoa."

Makoa's eyes widened. "How is it you know about me?"

"Last night six warriors from your village were brought to my village," she said, still fussing with the bandage knot. "The leader, a giant of a man, told our Chief and the kahuna what you had done."

"Then why do you not turn away from me in shame?"

Makaola was a long time in answering. "Would you turn away from me if I had broken a kapu and was hurting?" Her voice matched the beauty of her face.

"But you are good to look upon," Makoa said, "and no kapu could change that."

Makaola smiled. "And that might be the same reason I have not turned away from you, Makoa."

Her words pleased Makoa very much.

"Now be still while I loosen this knot."

"Did you know I was here?" Makoa asked.

"No, I come here as often as I can. This is my secret place...a place to think and dream."

"I call it Little Paradise," Makoa said.

"That is a good name for it," Makaola agreed. "I call it the Place of Talking Waters."

Makoa nodded. "That is also a good name for it."

As soon as Makaola removed the bandage, she gasped. "Oh, Makoa, your wound is badly infected!"

"It is nothing but a scratch," he said in warrior fashion.

"It is more than a scratch," she said, "and if it is not treated immediately, you will lose your arm or maybe even..."

"It cannot be that bad," Makoa protested lamely.

Makaola said nothing as she felt his forehead. Her knitted brow told Makoa more than he wanted to know.

"Makoa, I want you to get into the pool. I will help you."

"But the water is cold and my body is on fire."

"And that is why you must get in the water. Your body needs to be cooled, and quickly."

When he hesitated, Makaola chided him, "Are all the boys from your village afraid of cold water?"

Makoa stuck his chest out with a warrior's pride. "My name means fearless. I am not afraid of anything," he lied. Then, with teeth tightly clenched, Makoa threw himself into the cold water. Although the shock was much worse than the dagger stab from the boar, he did not cry out.

While he was in the pool, Makaola used a twig from a fern frond to clean his wound. Her fingers worked so tenderly that he scarcely felt any pain. Afterwards she bound his wound, using a strip from her cape.

"Your wound needs to be cleansed with coconut soap and the infection needs a poultice to draw out the poison. I must go back to my village to get these things. While I am gone, I want you to lie still and think only of pleasant things."

"I will do as you say," Makoa promised.

Cupping his fevered head with her cool hands, Makaola said, "I will return to you as quickly as I can." She smiled and then hurried away, disappearing into the thick foliage like a spirit.

Makoa did as Makaola had instructed him. He thought only of pleasant things: Makaola's almond shaped eyes, her graceful movements, the sound of her musical voice, the cool touch of her slender hands. And after dwelling on her many charms for a long time, Makoa's attention was drawn to the gurgling waterfall. Makaola called her secret place the Place of Talking Waters. Makoa strained to hear if the waters had words for him. After a long patient wait, the water seemed to say: 'You will live, you will live, you will live.' But when a dark rain cloud blocked out the sun and a stiff wind rustled the leaves, the waters seemed to chant, 'You must die, you must die, you must die!'

"No!" Makoa shouted, "I will live, I will live, I will live!" So saying, he collapsed into a troubled sleep.

The Pig Eater's village was about three miles from Makaola's Place of Talking Waters. Since she had been gone a long time, she knew her family and friends would be missing her. As soon as she reached her village, she quickly joined the celebration of the local god, which was in full progress. She danced the hula for awhile, then took part in a chase game. When her family and friends saw her laughing, dancing and playing games, they were reassured.

Although she appeared to be enjoying herself, Makaola was anxious to get back to Makoa. As she feigned interest in the festivities, she noticed Makoa's pursuers were doing the same. Like her, they would much rather be on their way to Makoa...but for very different reasons

When she was certain everyone had seen her, Makaola slipped away to her house. She collected her grandmother's strongest poultice along with some coconut soap, poi, dried banana chips, dried fish and a clean loincloth belonging to her oldest brother. After wrapping this in kapa cloth, she tied the bundle to her right calf. Her long cape would conceal it all. She waited anxiously until everyone was dancing, then sneaked away toward her place of talking waters, Makoa's Little Paradise.

'AHIKU
(SEVEN)

⌄⌃⌄⌃⌄⌃⌄⌃⌄⌃⌄⌃⌄⌃⌄

HEALTHY AGAIN

⌄⌃⌄⌃⌄⌃⌄⌃⌄⌃⌄⌃⌄⌃⌄

Concerned more for Makaola's safety than his own well being, Makoa worried about the girl's long absence. He sat propped against a tree, staring at the exact spot Makaola had exited the clearing. Still burning up with fever, he forced himself to stay awake—fearful that if he fell asleep something terrible would happen to her.

"What if a wild boar...perhaps the same one that attacked me..." Makoa shook the thought from his head.

"Makaola told me to think only of pleasant things," he reminded himself. And so he thought of Makaola. His mind pictures of her were of a smiling, laughing and teasing Makaola—a girl too beautiful and happy to be in any danger.

Keeping his eyes fixed on one spot made Makoa sleepy. His head began to bob up and down. Just as his chin settled on his chest, he heard a rustling noise in the thick foliage. His head snapped up straight.

"Is it the boar again?" he asked himself.

While his eyes searched the foliage, his right hand groped for the war club. When he found it, he stumbled to his feet, raising the club high above his head. Once up, however, he felt unsteady and terribly weak.

'You are going to die,' the waters seemed to murmur, 'You are going to die, you are going to die...'

As the noise in the bushes grew louder, Makoa was convinced the talking waters were right. He was going to die...and very soon it appeared. Just as his eyes clouded up, he saw a blurred image emerge from the surrounding forest. Was it the boar? His pursuers? Or his beautiful friend, Makaola?

This was the first time Makaola had ever seen Makoa standing. She was surprised at his height, almost as tall as a canoe paddle. He stood on wobbly legs, brandishing the war club at her and wavering back and forth. She could tell by his eyes he was delirious.

"Fear not, Makoa. It is me, Makaola."

On hearing her voice, Makoa lowered the war club.

"Makaola, Makaola," he whispered and then collapsed to the ground.

Moving quickly, Makaola dragged Makoa's limp body into the pool with her. She removed the bandage from his arm, then scrubbed his wound with coconut soap. Revived by the cool water, Makoa attempted to get out of the pool, but Makaola held on to him.

"No, no, Makoa. You must stay in the water until the fire in your body is cooled."

Reluctantly, he stayed in the pool until she decided it was time to get out. After drying his body with leaves, she applied a poultice to the boar wound.

"This will draw out the poison," she explained, "the poison that is setting your body on fire."

She used a wide shiny leaf for a dressing, then wrapped it with a strip of kapa cloth.

"And now, Makoa, you must eat something and drink much water...so much that your stomach will hurt."

Makoa wagged his head, "I am neither hungry nor thirsty, Makaola."

"But your body needs food for strength. And since you have lost much blood, you need much water to replace it."

She pointed a long slender finger in front of his face. "I insist you eat and drink. Do not waste my time by shaking your head at me!"

Makoa was too weak to resist her. She fed him banana chips and dried fish. Then she forced him to drink so much water his stomach felt like it would burst.

"This is for your own good," she kept saying.

But in his condition, Makoa found that hard to believe.

And then for the rest of the afternoon, Makaola nursed him. When his body trembled with chills, she covered him with her cape. When his body burned like a luau oven, she bathed him with cool water. She mopped his brow. She held his hand. She encouraged him with smiles and soft words.

Then, when long purple shadows covered Little Paradise, she said to him, "I must go back to my village now or my parents will come looking for me. Stay where you are until I return in the morning."

After brushing his forehead with her cheeks, she hurried away.

Until the moon was high overhead, Makoa tossed and turned as if a great battle was raging inside his body. And then all of a sudden...he felt a sense of peace and relief. He was neither hot nor chilled but comfortable enough to fall into a sound restful sleep.

A forest of kukui torches illuminated Makaola's village when she returned. The feast day of the Pig Eater's god was still going strong. People were singing, dancing, playing games and feasting. Makaola had not been missed. She joined the festivities, but went to her bed early so she could rise with the sun.

After a big feast day, most of the villagers would sleep until the sun set the following day. But would Makoa's pursuers sleep that long, Makaola wondered.

Her question was answered at daybreak. As she sneaked from the village, she saw Mookini and his warriors enter the temple to pray. She knew it would only be a short time before the pursuers would be on Makoa's trail.

Makaola wore a short kapa skirt so she would move quickly and freely. She hurried to Makoa as fast as she could. When she arrived at Little Paradise, she found him dressed in her brother's clean loincloth, sitting cross legged and eating banana chips.

"Aloha!" she greeted him. "You are looking much better than last time I saw you."

"Aloha! I am feeling much better than when you last saw me. And I owe it all to you. Mahalo, Makaola."

She bowed slightly. "It pleases me to help you. I am very happy to see you so full of life. But now I must tell you some bad news. Your pursuers are at this very moment searching for you. Do you feel well enough to travel?"

"I still feel a little weak, but fear of a crushed head will give me strength." He made light of it by laughing, but Makaola did not share his humor.

"Do not joke about such things, Makoa."

When he saw tears in her eyes, he stammered, "I...I am sorry."

"You must go now, Makoa. Your pursuers cannot be far behind. But first—I want to give you this for good luck." She placed an amulet around his neck bearing a green stone tiki image, the size of a baby's fist.

Makoa shook his head, "I cannot accept this gift, Makaola."

"Why not?" she asked, with hurt in her voice.

"Because I have nothing to give you in return."

Makaola smiled mischievously, "Good! Now you will be in my debt."

"But how can I ever repay you? I am marked for death."

"I have faith in you, Makoa." She placed her hand over his heart. "I am certain you will reach the Place of Refuge. And, I am confident that one day the spirit of the dead king, whose club you took, will forgive you. When that day comes, I will expect something from you,"

"I will never forget you, Makaola."

"I hope and pray you do not," she said. "Now you must hurry and go."

"Yes, but you must leave first. I need to buy time with still another trick for my pursuers." Without a word, Makaola threw her arms around Makoa's neck and hugged him. Then she ran from Little Paradise, choosing a different route home.

For a brief moment, Makoa stared with a heavy heart at the spot where Makaola had departed. Using a bundle of ferns as a broom, he erased all tracks made by Makaola, leaving those of the boar and himself. Then he hurried to begin his plan.

After ripping his blood stained loincloth to shreds, he threw the pieces next to the pool, alongside the blood soaked ground. With critical eyes, he surveyed the clearing until satisfied everything looked right. He secured his belongings and then backed out of Little Paradise, erasing his departing tracks with the fern broom. The sun was still young when he headed for the place of refuge.

'AWALU
(EIGHT)

CAPTURED

After leaving the temple, Mookini and his warriors went directly to the point where they had been intercepted by the Pig Eaters. In the time it would take to fast walk a mile, they picked up Makoa's trail. They followed it straight to his Little Paradise.

"Auwe!" one of the warriors shouted when he saw Makoa's blood stained loincloth.

"Come look!" he pointed. "Something terrible must have happened to the boy!"

Another warrior, the one called Lazy Eyelids, shouted, "Look at all of these hoof prints. A wild boar has surely killed Makoa!"

"And up here!" the shortest of the warriors cried, as he perched on top of the rock wall.

"There is blood all over this place!"

"Makoa must have tried to escape but failed," someone said.

Lazy Eyelids grinned. "It appears that this boar has fulfilled our mission for us...eh, Mookini?"

Mookini surprised everyone when he burst out laughing. He laughed so hard, he had to hold on to his sides for fear they would split wide open.

"What is so funny?" they all asked him.

"You!" he said as he continued to laugh. "All of you. You are funnier than any joke I have ever heard."

"How is that, Mookini?" Lazy Eyelids asked.

"You are all so quick to believe such skimpy signs," Mookini replied, wiping the tears from his eyes.

"What do you mean by that? It is as clear as lagoon water what has happened here. A wild boar killed the one we chased...Makoa."

With grunts and nodding heads, the other warriors agreed with Lazy Eyelids.

"That is exactly what Makoa wants you to believe," Mookini said, "and he has succeeded."

"But what about the blood stained malo?"

"What about the blood stained ground?"

"And these prints. Are they not those of a boar? And a huge one at that?"

Mookini shook his head indulgently. "Yes, yes, they are real enough. And I am sure some kind of fight took place here. But if a boar killed Makoa, as you all seem to think, then where are the boy's bones?"

"He carried them away," someone said.

"In a gourd jug?" Mookini asked innocently, " Or perhaps in a woven palm basket fashioned by his sow wife...eh?"

The warriors shuffled their feet as they eyed one another.

"And then there is the war club," Mookini continued. "Did the boar carry that away also? Perhaps to use in battle after he loses his tusks to old age? Eh, what about that?"

When they didn't answer, Mookini chided them.

"This boy has already tricked you twice. Are you so eager to be tricked a third time?"

Feeling foolish, the warriors hung their heads in shame.

Mookini spat on the blood stained loincloth.

"We have wasted enough time on this trick. Let us fan out like palm fronds and search for Makoa's trail."

Although the fever had left him, Makoa still

felt the effects of it. Every muscle in his body ached, especially those in his legs. He had to stop frequently to rest and rub the cramps from his calves. Because of these many rest periods, it took him the better part of a day to skirt the northern edge of the volcano, Mauna Loa. Eager as he was to put time and distance between the pursuers and himself, Makoa thanked the eyeball God of the Sun for closing its eyes.

Before total darkness covered the land, Makoa made a hasty camp in a small grove of stiff-limbed trees. He was so exhausted he fell into a sound sleep, despite the mournful humming of the war club.

He would not have slept so soundly had he known that at that very moment his pursuers were only a dozen javelin throws away...

▚▽▚▽▚▽▚▽▚▽

As usual, Makoa had covered his tracks well. But Mookini was no novice to tracking down kapu breakers. After leaving Little Paradise, his trained eye detected a faint set of Makoa's footprints.

"Over here!" He yelled to the others, "Come and see! Makoa has passed this way!"

On hands and knees, Mookini studied the ground. After crawling the length of a war canoe, he stood up with a grin on his face.

"The boy is not moving like he did before. The space between each footprint is shorter... Makoa is tiring."

"Perhaps he is tired from his fight with the boar," Lazy Eyelids said with a smirk.

"It may be that his wounds are draining his energy," another added. The short warrior clicked his tongue, "...and after losing so much blood..."

Mookini gave each warrior a hard look.

"You say these things to shorten me. I have already agreed that Makoa fought with a boar. What is important is that the boar did not kill him. See for yourself." He pointed to the tracks with his spear point. "Those are the prints of Makoa...a live Makoa."

Lazy Eyelids smiled weakly at Mookini, "We did not mean to embarrass you."

"Ka!" He said scornfully, "I am no fool. But in your attempt to embarrass me, you only make yourself look foolish. And I will prove that when we catch up with Makoa. Now enough of this silly bird chatter. If we hurry, we can overtake that kapu breaker by the time the goddess in the moon shows herself."

And so it had happened that way. While Makoa's feet were taking short, stingy steps, his pursuers were flying along the ground with giant strides. Just before reaching the small grove of stiff-limbed trees, a full moon rose to guide the warriors to Makoa's camp.

Quietly they surrounded the boy's sleeping body. Mookini pointed to the movements of Makoa's chest with the point of his spear.

"See," he whispered softly, "Makoa is alive and breathing the same as you and me."

The warriors nodded, then erected four torch poles—one for each direction on earth. Shortly after they lit the torches, Makoa's eyes opened. At first he thought he was looking into the face of a Tiki God with fierce eyes, snarling mouth and tattooed cheeks. Makoa could only scream inside himself. His tongue was stiffened like cooled lava.

"Praying to the spirit of the dead?" Mookini asked.

Makoa nodded, for that was exactly what he was doing.

"Fear not, trickster. You are not dead...yet. But you will be as soon as we take you home. And we will start back when the sun first shows itself."

Makoa sighed. It was useless to resist. Silently, he placed his fate in the hands of the gods.

Without a word, the warriors bound Makoa's hands and feet with vines from the stiff limbed trees. They tied so many tight knots in his bonds that it would be impossible to loosen them with just teeth and fingers. While Makoa lay helpless on his back, Mookini approached him, hefting his long 10-foot throwing spear in his right hand and wearing a sinister smile.

"Makoa, you have caused us much trouble with your tricks. To keep you from moving about and causing mischief, I will leave my spear to guard you."

With both hands Mookini lifted his long spear, holding it straight up and down. Makoa's face turned to stone. Then with a mighty grunt, Mookini plunged the spear blade between Makoa's legs and deep into the ground.

"Auwe!" Makoa yelled, causing the warriors to break out laughing.

To further strengthen the position of the spear, Mookini leaped onto the shaft, driving the spear still deeper into the ground.

"That should pen you for tonight!" Mookini said, wiping his hands together.

Impressed by what Mookini had done, the warriors hooted and slapped their thighs like rowdy children. Makoa could not close his ears to their taunts, but he could and did close his eyes to the crazy faces they made at him.

When they tired of poking fun at Makoa, the

warriors prepared a quick supper for themselves.

While the warriors ate, Mookini took a leaf tray of food to Makoa and sat next to him. As he hand fed the boy, he questioned him.

"How did you learn all those tricks you played on us!"

"I learned them while playing the hunter and hunted game," Makoa replied.

"Mmmmmm. It is too bad you broke such a great kapu. You would have made a great warrior. Not as good as me," he smiled, "but almost."

When Mookini smiled, his face did not look so fiercesome to Makoa.

"Tell me," Mookini said, pointing to Makoa's bandaged arm. "Who was it that took care of your wound?"

Caught off guard, Makoa stammered, "Uh, uh, I did it myself."

Mookini laughed. "Ha, Makoa! The design on the kapa bandage is not of our village. But I have seen that pattern before...in the village of the Pig Eaters."

Makoa sighed. Mookini was much too smart to be lied to.

"Yes, someone from that village did help me. But I will not tell you who it was! Never!"

Mookini rose to his feet with a wide grin on his tattooed face.

"And I will not ask you her name. Never!"

Surprised, Makoa snapped, "How did you know it was a girl?"

"Only a kahuna or a girl in love could have put such a neat bandage on your arm. A kahuna would have turned you over to us. A girl in love would keep it a secret. Besides that," Mookini winked, "the design on your kapa bandage is the same kind worn by the females in the village of the Pig Eaters...Rest well, Makoa."

After eating, the warriors entertained themselves by telling adventure stories. And when the torches had burned down to tiny flames, each man curled up next to a tree and fell asleep. Makoa waited a long time before he tried to pull the spear from the ground. But the spear was embedded so deeply, he could not budge it at all. He tried to break it by pulling and pushing against it, but the shaft was made of a very hard wood. It would bend a little but not break.

Since he could not loosen his bonds, nor break or pull the spear from the ground, Makoa had but one chance left. He had to climb up the spear far enough to get one leg over the top of it.

With the aid of the spear he pulled himself to his feet. It was an awkward position at best. Makoa had to hold on tightly to the spear lest he fall backwards. The top of the spear seemed just a short distance away. But each time Makoa tried to pull himself up the highly polished wood, his hands would slide down as if smeared with coconut oil. His feet, on the opposite side of the spear, were of no use whatsoever. After a dozen futile attempts to climb the slippery spear, Makoa gave up.

Exhausted and discouraged, Makoa sank to the ground. As he toyed with the green stone god image, he thought, "Makaola gave me this talisman for good luck. Ha! My luck so far has been all bad."

While he fingered the talisman he noticed that although the face and back of the god image were polished smooth, the edges were left rough. Encouraged, Makoa inserted one end of the stone in his mouth clenching it tightly with his teeth. Then he sawed the vine ropes that bound his hands back and forth on the rough edges of the talisman.

The faint grating noise seemed loud when magnified by the still night air. He had to stop each time a warrior stirred in his sleep. It took a long, hard, nerve-racking time to free his hands. While working on his feet bonds, he grew impatient and sawed with too much enthusiasm. The warrior nearest him turned over with his face toward Makoa. It was too dark for Makoa to see the man's eyes. He couldn't tell if the warrior was watching him or not. Makoa waited, without

sawing, for what seemed a very long time. And then, when he heard the warrior snoring, he went back to his sawing.

With the last of the bonds cut, Makoa clamped a hand over his mouth for fear he might cry out with joy. Then, after composing himself, he picked up the kapu war club where he had first placed it. (The warriors had not dared to touch it.)

Quietly he tiptoed past the warriors, stopping by Mookini's sleeping body. The leader's knife, a beautiful weapon of polished wood and volcanic glass, lay next to his side. Makoa picked it up . . . thinking how easy it would be to kill Mookini as he slept. Then perhaps the rest of the warriors would lose heart and give up the chase.

But these were only fanciful thoughts. Makoa knew in his heart he could not kill Mookini in such a way. The warrior was only doing his duty and Makoa admired him for that. He returned the knife, sticking the volcanic glass blade into the ground near Mookini's head. Without a sound, Makoa disappeared into the night with his feet moving toward the leeward side of the island.

'AIWA
(NINE)

ESCAPE

Moonlight enabled Makoa to travel during most of the night. Still suffering the effects of his bout with fever, he stopped many times to rest. By the time the sun showed itself, Makoa was too tired to continue the chase game. He crawled under the first fern bush he saw and fell asleep.

"Auwe!" Lazy Eyelids shouted, "Makoa has escaped! Wake up, everyone, wake up!"

When Mookini's eyes opened, the first thing he saw was his knife, stuck in the ground just inches from his head. "No doubt," he thought, "the boy did that to prove he had the opportunity to kill me."

As he prepared to give chase, Mookini puzzled over the knife. "Why did he not kill me...why?"

But when he was fully awake and realized that Lazy Eyelids had seen the knife stuck near his head, Mookini felt humiliated, then angry, and finally vindictive.

"Let us give chase to that outlaw, that mischief maker!" he growled. "Wikiwiki!"

A cramp in his right calf brought Makoa out of a deep sleep. He jumped to his feet and hopped around in a circle until the knot in his muscle was loosened. As he massaged his leg, his eyes searched the sky for a sign of time. But the sun was well hidden by low hanging clouds, heavy with rain. His best guess was noontime. The long rest had put new life into Makoa. Without taking time for a seated meal, he ate dried fish and fruit as he ran.

Like Makoa, Mookini and his warriors ate on the run. The rain clouds were soon accompanied by cool trade winds that kept the pursuers fresh and eager. All day long, with only short rest periods, the pursuers stayed on the boy's trail. To keep his throwing arm in shape, Mookini would hurl his long spear at a tree well ahead of him. His target was always a slim tree about the width of Makoa's body. Before making night camp, Mookini had thrown his spear many times. Not once did he fail to hit his target dead center. Only one warrior believed Mookini had a magic arm. The rest claimed he had a magic spear.

Although Makoa made good time before stopping for the night, his pursuers had made better time. And when a hot sun peeked its eye on the hunters and the hunted, they were all running.

Makoa had no way of knowing that his pursuers were closing the distance between them. But for some strange, mysterious reason, he knew they were getting closer with every passing moment. Before the morning was half spent, he saw several sea birds soaring overhead—an obvious sign that the coast was not far away. Realizing he would have to head south soon in order to reach the Pu'uhonua, he felt it necessary to slow the pursuers with one final trick. He stopped running to arrange it.

"Look, Mookini!" A warrior shouted as he pointed to the sky. "Sea birds!"

"Yes, and that means our friend Makoa will soon have to head south. Keep a sharp lookout, all of you!"

No sooner were the words out of the leader's mouth when an advance scout shouted back to him.

"Look, Mookini! A sign...no, two signs. Over here! Over here!"

On one knee Mookini examined the two trails made by Makoa.

"Ah ha! The boy is up to his old tricks."

"Yes," Lazy Eyelids agreed. "Look how he has marked an easy to follow trail to the south and a hard to follow one to the north."

"Just as he did near the village of the banana eaters." The tall warrior added.

Then all at once and at the same time, the warriors voiced their opinions.

"I think this time we should follow the obvious trail..."

"Yes, remember how he fooled us last..."

"No! That is what he wants us to do, I think..."

"He went north. I'm sure of it. Then he backtracked..."

"Hold your tongues!" Mookini roared. "I cannot think with all that squawking in my ears!"

The warriors grew silent as Mookini rubbed his chin in deep thought. When he spoke, his words were slow and deliberate.

"We have no time to waste trying to out-guess Makoa." He then broke them into pairs. "You two head south; you two head north. Lazy Eyelids and I will continue west."

"But there is no sign of a trail going west," the tall one argued.

"And it is about time for Makoa to turn south if he wishes to reach the Pu'uhonua," another added.

"If he can backtrack to the north, and the south, he can surely backtrack to the west," Mookini countered, "and as to the time for heading south...well, the coast is still a little time away."

His piercing eyes panned their faces. "Now will you obey me or not?" He hefted the long magical spear in his hand. "What say you?"

Right away the short warrior fell to his knees and prayed aloud:

"O Great Goddess, Pele,
the fish are waiting, the
baked pig is waiting, the
wife is waiting, the
children are waiting.
Help us to catch Makoa,
Then carry us home

on the wings of swift birds.
My prayer is delivered,
my prayer is received...pau   (finished)."

"And so is the talk," Mookini snapped. "Now back to the chase! Back to the chase!"

◢◣◥◤◢◣◥◤◢◣◥◤

With the crisp, clean smell of the sea in his nostrils, Makoa raced to a bluff overlooking the Pu'uhonua. It was just as his village kahuna had described so many times in his lectures: 'A slender arm of land sticking out into the sea, a 12-foot high wall of tight fitting lava blocks guarding its land shoulder, several thatched huts for housing priests and guards, and one large wooden temple to make the place sacred.'

All in all, the Pu'uhonua was not an impressive sight. Even so, this humble place possessed the power to forgive and protect any kapu breaker from the wrath of any king or kahuna.

Except for several tall wooden god images that stared menacingly out at the open sea, the seaward sides of the six acre spit of sand and palm trees were left unprotected. For awhile Makoa wondered about this until his attention was drawn to the rock wall.

Standing side by side with the Pu'uhonua guards stood men from his own village...on the lookout for the great kapu breaker, Makoa.

"No time to feel sorry for myself," Makoa murmured. With his eyes toward the sea, for this was his only hope, he moved northward. When he reached another spit of land, several hundred yards above the refuge, he scrambled down the bluff and onto the beach. His plan was simple—find something to float on, then head for Pu'uhonua's unprotected arm.

As Makoa combed the beach, he spied the broken section of a surf board sticking up out of the sand. Like a dog digging up a bone he pawed at the sand until he uncovered a 6-foot piece, long enough to carry him across the small bay.

Just when he thought the gods were smiling on him, a long dark shadow fell over him. When he looked up to see what caused the shadow, he saw Mookini and Lazy Eyelids staring at him from the edge of the bluff.

Quickly Makoa ran toward the water, the war club stuck in his waistband and the surf board held high above his head. Mookini leaped to the sandy beach, poised to throw his spear as soon as he landed. Lazy Eyelids scrambled down much the same way Makoa had. With his left arm aimed at Makoa's back and his muscular legs spread well apart, Mookini hefted the spear in his right hand.

Before Makoa reached the water's edge,

Mookini let fly his magical spear. Like a song bird it whistled through the air. Judging from its path, Lazy Eyelids was totally confident it would find its mark.

The hairs on the back of Makoa's neck were standing out stiff as boar bristles. In his heart he knew Mookini's spear point would soon slice into his body just as easily as it would a baked milk fish.

And then, to Makoa's amazement, and also that of Lazy Eyelids, Mookini's magical spear hit the beach . . . a full spear's length short of Makoa's fleeing body!

When he heard the spear blade swish into the sand directly behind him, Makoa stopped. He turned to stare at Mookini in wonderment. The warrior stared back with a stoic expression. Both puzzled and relieved, Makoa entered the water lying face down on the surf board. Then, using his hands and feet as paddles, he headed for the northern shore line of the Place of Refuge.

"Ka! Mookini, now I have seen everything," Lazy Eyelids scoffed. "The greatest spear thrower in all of Pele's Island has just missed a target that a young boy could have easily hit!"

With such words, Lazy Eyelids feared he would certainly evoke Mookini's anger. But again, Mookini surprised Lazy Eyelids by falling to his knees and laughing so hard he shook like he had fever chills. After scratching his head a few times, Lazy Eyelids fell to his knees and laughed just as hard as his leader.

As Makoa neared the palm lined beach, he caught sight of the steep roof lines of the sacred temple. With no wall guarding the seaward side, Makoa figured he would be safe within a very short time. While he was thinking how easy this part of his journey was turning out to be, he saw something that struck fear in every nerve of his body. The dorsal fins of three large tiger sharks suddenly appeared above a patch of dark green water.

"Auwe!" he moaned, "Lua Mano!" (den of the shark!)

And then be vaguely remembered the village kahuna mentioning this in one of his lectures...a lecture during which Makoa had daydreamed.

It was now perfectly clear why the seaward side of the Pu'uhonua was not walled...there was no need of a wall...not with sharks around!

One of the sharks turned and came straight for Makoa. The other two then followed close behind. As fast as he could, Makoa churned the water while pulling with his hands and kicking with his feet. His flailing body, however, excited the sharks all the more and they cruised in on him with great speed.

When the lead shark was about twenty yards

from him, Makoa withdrew the kapu war club from his waistband. Lifting it high above his head, he yelled a fierce war cry. Then as the lead shark closed in, Makoa's eyes widened at the sight – terrifying jaws armed with rows of knife-sharp teeth – lifeless eyes, black as obsidian – a devil god intent on devouring him.

With the courage of a war god, Makoa whacked the monster on its snout as hard as he could... just as he had whacked the wild boar.

Bright red blood spurted from the wound, darkening still further the deep green water of Lua Mano. Drawn by the blood scent, the other two sharks targeted their brother instead of Makoa. And while they attacked the wounded shark, Makoa paddled safely to the tiny crescent beach of the Pu'uhonua.

'UMI
(TEN)

FORGIVENESS

When Makoa reached shore, the chief kahuna came down from the temple to greet him. He wore a richly decorated loincloth and a long red cape. His head was crowned with a feathered helmet...similar to that worn by warrior chiefs.

"Aloha," he said in a very deep voice. "Why have you come here?"

Afraid, but standing tall, Makoa replied, "I have broken a great kapu."

"What kapu have you broken?" the kahuna asked. Makoa showed the war club to the priest.

"I took this from a king's burial place."

With narrowed eyes, the chief kahuna stared at the club. It was a long time before he spoke. "Did you not know that it was kapu to even enter a king's burial place?"

"Yes, kahuna."

"And did you not know that it was kapu to even touch anything that belonged to a king?"

"Yes, kahuna."

"Then why did you do such things?" The kahuna asked.

"Because I did not think wisely."

"Tell me, when did you start thinking wisely?"

Makoa looked the priest straight in the eye. "When Pele punished my village by spilling lava."

"Why did you not then put the club back with its spirit?" asked the kahuna.

"I tried to put it back," explained Makoa, "but a lava flow covered the cave entrance before I had a chance to return it."

"Mmmmm, you have indeed broken a great kapu," the kahuna said with a grave voice.

Makoa lowered his head in shame and replied, "Yes, and I am truly sorry."

"Tell me, Makoa, what do you expect to find here?" the priest asked.

"I seek refuge and forgiveness," Makoa replied.

"Refuge I can offer you because this is a place of refuge and no one can harm you while you are here. As for forgiveness, I usually absolve the lawbreaker within a day or two. But your situation is different. You still have the king's club and Pele has sealed his tomb preventing you from returning it. It would seem that Pele and the king's spirit do not want you to be forgiven so quickly."

The kahuna then took Makoa by the hand and led him into the Sacred Temple.

"Place the war club on the altar," he ordered, "and confess your crime."

Makoa placed the club on the altar stone, then related his story to the priest. He told him all about the cave. He told him about his village's troubles because of him. He told him about his fight with the wild boar and the tiger sharks. He told him about his experiences with the pursuers and Makaola. The kahuna listened carefully and with great interest. When Makoa finished, the priest smiled and said, "Then the blood stains on the war club belong to a killer shark...is that correct?"

"Yes, kahuna."

"Then I am sure," the Priest said, "that in time Pele will forgive you. And I am equally sure the spirit that owns the war club will forgive you. If the spirit wished you dead, he would not have allowed his club to save you against the boar and the shark."

Makoa breathed a deep sigh of relief. "I will do anything to be forgiven by Pele and the spirit of the club...and also my village."

Pleased with Makoa's words, the kahuna laid a hand on the boy's shoulder. "Then you must stay here in the Pu'uhonua until there is a sign of forgiveness. While you are here, you will serve the temple and wonder about life and the ways of the gods."

True to the kahuna's direction, Makoa served the temple. Each day he swept the floor clean. He fashioned mats out of hala leaves for the sanctuary. He made sure the lamps were always filled with oil from the kukui nut. And when he was not busy with these chores, he helped the temple priests carve fierce god images that stood inside and outside the temple.

Despite a busy schedule, Makoa did have time to wonder about many things. Why, for instance, did the savage-like Mookini throw his spear short, thus sparing his life and allowing him to escape? He wondered if Pele would ever forgive him — or would he spend the rest of his life in this Place of Refuge? Would the dead king's spirit forgive him and allow him to return the war club? Would his village then claim him as their own — or ban him forever from their midst?

But mostly he wondered about Makaola, especially when he walked along the beach each evening. Would she wait for him, saving her love for him and him alone?

To match her gift of the green stone talisman, he collected tiny shells during his walks. When he had collected three large calabashes of shells, he selected one shell that pleased his eyes in size, shape and color. Using this shell as a model, he painstakingly culled the ones that did not match it. He then strung the chosen shells on a palm fiber string. The finished product was a necklace of shells, perfectly matched in size, shape and color.

When Makoa was not thinking of Makaola, time passed swiftly enough, but when his mind was filled with her, time passed like a walking sea turtle.

And then one day, after a year had almost passed, a messenger from Makoa's village arrived at the Pu'uhonua. He whispered something in the chief kahuna's ear which caused the priest to smile.

"There is good news for you, Makoa. An earth tremor has broken away the lava crust that covered your kapu cave. This is a sign that Pele has forgiven you and the spirit of the dead king is giving you a chance to return his club!"

"Pele be praised!" Makoa shouted, "This is good news indeed."

So saying, he fell to his knees and thanked

the kahuna. Then he ran to the temple and prostrated himself before the altar. For a long time he prayed, scarcely believing his good fortune. Afterwards, he wrapped the war club in kapa cloth and said goodbye to the chief kahuna.

"Aloha, O great kahuna! Mahalo, mahalo."

"You have used your wit to escape punishment for breaking a kapu, Makoa. Now use that same wit to keep from breaking a kapu."

Then the kahuna absolved Makoa of his crime and blessed him: "Hele me ka hau 'oli." (Go with joy.)

The shortest way back to his village was a path that skirted Mauna Loa and Kilauea to the south. But so anxious was Makoa to see Makaola that he headed north to the two volcanoes using the same path he had trod on his way to the Place of Refuge. With just short naps he travelled day and night. When he reached Little Paradise, he found a small shrine at the exact spot Makaola had nursed him. Judging from the flower and food remains, his "happy" girl had visited the shrine often. By those same remains, however, Makoa could tell she hadn't been to Little Paradise in a long time. Had she given up on him?

Desperate to find out, Makoa detoured to

visit her village. But Makaola was not there . . . and to make matters worse, no one would tell him where she had gone.

With a heavy heart, Makoa set his feet toward his own village. All the rainbow joy he felt at being forgiven of his kapu was suddenly storm clouded by the loss of Makaola.

Two days later, as he neared his village, his heart was lightened somewhat by the familiar tapping sounds of kapa making. Tired as he was, he rushed toward those sounds until he came upon four young women whose faces he recognized. Using wooden mallets they were pounding strips of the inner bark of the paper mulberry tree into kapa cloth.

The first to see Makoa jumped up and yelled, "Auwe! It is Makoa, back from the Place of Refuge...back from the dead!"

She then ran to the temple to tell the kahuna. The other young women presented him with a water filled gourd to cleanse himself and then a drinking coconut for refreshment.

By the time Makoa reached the temple, word of his presence had spread throughout the village. Everyone was there to witness his meeting with the kahuna. As he passed through their ranks, he spied his father and mother. They both had tears in their eyes but were smiling like little children. Makoa was tempted to run to them but he stifled the urge. His first responsibility was to present himself to the kahuna and then return the club. He returned his parents' smile, but then made his face serious as he knelt before the kahuna.

In a loud voice for all to hear, the priest cried, "Makoa, you are indeed a fortunate young man. Pele has forgiven you by breaking the same lava crust she sent to seal your doom. With gratitude in your heart, return now the war club you took from the burial cave!"

Makoa bowed to the kahuna, then was escorted to the cliff by the very same warriors that had pursued him. The villagers followed close behind.

With ropes, a grim faced Mookini and his warriors lowered Makoa down to the cave. He entered, and without looking at the dead king, replaced the war club. He left the cave without looking back. As he was pulled up, the weight of guilt he had carried for almost a year was lifted from his shoulders.

"My joy would be complete," he thought, "if only Makaola..."

The first to congratulate him were his one time pursuers. Flashing big smiles, Mookini and his men slapped Makoa on the back and treated him as their equal. Makoa thanked Mookini for sparing his life – but the warrior feigned ignorance.

"It was just a bad spear throw," he insisted. But Makoa knew better.

After sharing warm alohas with his parents and his good friend, Kakani, his mother said, "We have a surprise for you, my son."

Then Makoa's father waved a hand toward the rear of the crowd.

Makoa couldn't believe his eyes. Makaola, more beautiful than he remembered, was walking toward him. Her eyes were dancing and she was smiling happily, just like her namesake. Without a word she crowned his head with a garland of fragrant leaves. In return, Makoa placed the necklace of matched shells around her neck saying, "When you gave me the green stone amulet, you said you would expect something from me the day when the spirit of the dead king forgave me...remember?"

"Yes," she murmured, "but I did not expect such a precious gift. The shells are perfectly matched." She ran her fingers over each one. "It is so...so beautiful."

Makoa was tempted to say, "not as beautiful as you." But afraid that his words might sound foolish, he merely grinned awkwardly at her. Kakani made it worse by batting his eyes at Makoa and grinning like he had lost his mind.

That night the village celebrated Makoa's

freedom with a big feast. It was the biggest and best luau Makoa had ever attended. The best portions of the kalua pig were given to him. And despite the promise he made to himself, to never eat pig again, he gorged himself on the succulent pork.

Everyone shared Makoa's joy with singing and much dancing. When Makaola performed a hula in front of Makoa, she transferred the red flower she wore behind her right ear to her left...directly over her heart. No words were necessary.

Makoa never forgot the big luau given in his honor. Nor did he ever forget the beautifully carved war club that had given him such short lived pleasure and long endured pain. He kept the memories in his heart and never broke another big kapu for as long as he lived.

PAU

GLOSSARY

Hawaiian Phrase　　Meaning
(Phonetic Pronunciation)

aloha　(ah-loh-ha):　　Greetings; welcome; farewell.

auwe　(ow-way):　　Exclamation; strong feeling;
too bad; woe is me.

hala　(hah-lah):　　Leaves of the pandanus tree;
used to make mats, baskets,
fans, etc.

heiau　(hay-ow):　　Ancient Hawaiian temple made
of stone or wood.

hula　(hoo-lah):　　Hawaiian dance.

kahuna
(kah-hoo-nah):　　Hawaiian priest, advisor, healer.

kalua
(kah-loo-ah) pig:　　A whole young pig wrapped in
leaves and baked in an
underground pit-oven.

kapa　(kah-pah):　　Cloth made from the inner
bark of the mamaki tree and
the paper mulberry tree.

91

kapu (kah-poo):   Sacred ban or law; an object, word or act protected by such law; something forbidden; a no-no.

koa (ko-a):   A tree whose hard wood is used for making canoes, carvings and tools.

Kona (koh-nah)
Coast: Stretch of coastline on leeward side of the Big Island, Hawaii.

kukui
(koo-koo-ee):   Candlenut tree. Nuts from this tree were used for roasting; oil used for lamps, torches.

leeward: Side of island sheltered from the wind.

lei (lay):   Necklace of flowers, leaves, shells or feathers.

luau (loo-ow):   A feast.

mahalo
(mah-hah-loh):   Thank you, thanks.

malo (ma-lo):   Short loin cloth worn by males.

Menehune
(men-eh-hoo-nay): Dwarf people; early ancestors; helpful forest spirits who built fish ponds, roads and temples.

monkey pod: Wood from the rain tree; used for bowls, carvings, dishes.

pau (pow): Finished; done.

poi (poy): A starchy food made from the taro plant; staple of Hawaiian diet.

tiki (tee-kee): In Polynesian mythology, the first man. Image of sorcery and good luck.

wahine
(wha-hee-nay): Woman; girl; female.

wikiwiki
(wee-kee-wee-kee): Quickly, very fast, hurry.

windward: Side of island exposed to the wind.